MORE GRAPHIC NOVELS AVAILABLE FROM

AMY'S DIARY #1 "SPACE ALIEN... ALMOST?"

AMY'S DIARY #2 "THE WORLD'S UPSIDE DOWN"

AMY'S DIARY #3 "MOVING ON"

STITCHED #1 "THE FIRST DAY OF THE REST OF HER LIFE"

STITCHED #2 "LOVE IN THE TIME OF ASSUMPTION"

CHLOE #1 "THE NEW GIRL"

CHLOE #2 "THE QUEEN OF HIGH SCHOOL"

CHLOE #3 "FRENEMIES"

CHLOE #4 "RAINY DAY"

ANA AND THE COSMIC RACE #1 "THE RACE BEGINS

SCARLET ROSE #1 "I KNEW I'D MEET YOU"

SCARLET ROSE #2 "I'LL GO WHERE YOU GO"

SCARLET ROSE #3 "I THINK I LOVE YOU"

SCARLET ROSE #4 "YOU WILL ALWAYS BE MINE"

G.F.F.s #1 "MY HEART LIES IN THE 90s"

G.F.F.s #2 "WITCHES GET THINGS DONE"

MONICA ADVENTURES #1

MONICA ADVENTURES #2

MONICA ADVENTURES #3

SWEETIES #1 "CHERRY SKYE"

SEE MORE AT PAPERCUTZ.COM

Amy's Diary

Diary

Moving On

Based on the novels by INDIA DESJARDINS

Adaptation — VÉRONIQUE GRISSEAUX

Illustration — LAËTITIA AYNIÉ

NEW YORK

Véronique and Laëtitia, a team on fire that's really captured Amy's world. Elsa Lafon, my accomplice overseas. Annabelle, Laetitia Lehmann, Mélanie Rouzière, Corinne De Vailly, and the whole Michel Lafon and Jungle teams.
—*India*

Thanks to Amy for making me live such a long, beautiful adventure with two talented authors and two awesome editors!
—*Laëtitia*

What a pleasure to have worked with you, Laëtitia!
Thanks to the awesome Jungle and Lafon team.
And especially a huuuuge thanks to India!
I love this Amy Von Brandt, I love her!
—*Véronique*

Amy's Diary

#3 "Moving On"
Le journal d'Aurélie Laflamme [AMY'S DIARY] volume 3 *"Ça Déménage"* © 2016 Jungle/Michel Lafon. All Rights Reserved. www.editions-jungle.com. Used under license.

Based on the novels by INDIA DESJARDINS
VÉRONIQUE GRISSEAUX—Comics Adaptation
LAËTITIA AYNIÉ—Art, Color, Design
JOE JOHNSON—Translation
BRYAN SENKA—Lettering
LÉA ZIMMERMAN—Production
IZZY BOYCE-BLANCHARD—Editorial Intern
JEFF WHITMAN—Managing Editor
JIM SALICRUP
Editor-in-Chief

Thanks to Véronique and Laetritia,
a team on fire that's really captured Amy's world.

Special thanks to FLORA BOFFY

Charmz is an imprint of Papercutz.
Papercutz.com

Hardcover ISBN: 978-1-5458-0344-8
Paperback ISBN: 978-1-5458-0345-5

Printed in China
November 2019

Distributed by Macmillan
First Charmz printing

- Friday, January 5th:

9:52am:

Everything's great!
(If I hadn't become hyper-aware about global warming and if I weren't worried about saving trees, I'd fill this page with exclamation marks to illustrate the true intensity of my happiness.)

Everything's going so great, I wonder if it can be possible to be this happy? So much so, I have nothing to talk about.

NOTHING!

Now I'm part of that category of happy people with no problems. That's new for me. Me, who so often feels like aliens abandoned me on Earth after an intergalactic voyage (yes, yes, apart from the fact that ET is truly ugly, I've identified with that character for a long time).

9:54am:

This morning, when I woke up, I turned on my new TV that I placed right in front of my bed. (The one I got for Christmas from my mom. I also got a super awesome present from my Granny Von Brandt: she gave me pictures of my dad to make a scrapbook of his life. That way he'll always be close to me!). So, back to TV... just in time for the music video I've been wanting to watch... Craaaazy!

And when I hit the "on" button and the video I was wanting to see popped up on my screen, I just knew it was going be a great day. That life was giving me exactly what I wanted right when I wanted it.

9:56am:

What can I fantasize about, now that all my dreams have come true? I know what I could do. I could dream of not being in a dentist's chair, with a dental hygienist energetically scratching away at my teeth with a scaler while, in the neighboring room, an instrument's making the sound zweeeee, zweeeeee, which is splitting my eardrums.

6

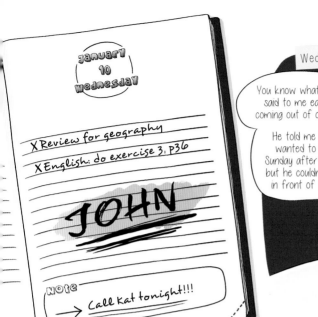

january 10 wednesday

X Review for geography
X English: do exercise 3, p36

JOHN

note
→ Call Kat tonight!!!

Wednesday, January 10th, 7:15pm

You know what John said to me earlier coming out of class...?

He told me he really wanted to kiss me Sunday after the game, but he couldn't do that in front of his coach.

And then he told me Frederica was his ex!

Whaaat?

Frederica, one of the 3 parakeets?

Kat, may I borrow your blue sweater?

Yeah. And... tatatataaa, John invited me to a movie and afterwards we're going over to his friends' Friday night!

JULIANNE, get out of my bedroom!

Stop digging around my closet! MOM!

Amy, I gotta go.

I don't know how I'll get any sleep. My heart's beating too fast. I can't wait for it to be Friday night!

9

Since it takes chewing gum years to biodegrade, future scientists could get traces of our DNA and clone us... So yes, it's the gum Nick was chewing and passed to me when we were kissing. Now that I have a new boyfriend and I can look at things, shall we say, more maturely, I don't need these future plans for cloning anymore... I agreed to toss the gum.

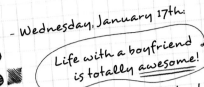

- Wednesday, January 17th:

Life with a boyfriend is totally <u>awesome!</u>

Everything seems lighter to me, different. Food is better. The floor doesn't look so hard. Jokes are funnier. The cold doesn't penetrate the pores of my skin...

(but using that argument with my mom as a reason for not wearing a hat is impossible).

Oh, my God! I'm an assassin!

I attempted unpremeditated murder!

But it's not your fault.

John is allergic to peanuts. You ate some peanut butter toast this morning, you kissed him on the lips, so here we are.

I don't dare think of what might have happened if I'd kissed him more, let's say... passionately!

Don't worry, I'm not mad at you I should've told you I was allergic.

I'm a horrible killer and I think John has Stockholm Syndrome.

Stockholm Syndrome:
Noun: Stockholm Syndrome is a complex psychological phenomenon (because it's paradoxical) of sympathy between the victim and his or her executioner.

11

So, I have a crush on BEN SENARD. He's a senior.

Boys our age are weaklings. You saw how your John nearly died just because you kissed him...

He had an allergic reaction!

Are you sure?

Boys our age are mutants, genetic errors...

Still, liking some guy you have to say "sir" to isn't ideal.

Honestly! He's just two years older.

I have a plan to meet him... After breakfast, Ben goes up to the 3rd floor to go to the library. I'll hide behind the restroom door that's beside it, as he's passing by, you'll signal me, I'll come out... and I'll run into him!

12:45pm

Oh! Ben... they're waiting for you in the French class.

Okay, that's a no-go!

Near the library, irritated by the failure of her plan, Kat passed by a boy our age or rather, in our grade, named Alex. He offered to sign her up for his science club. Kat instantly agreed. There's no need to be good in math to understand the equation:

→ Giving up on Ben + the desire to participate in the science club (although Kat hates science),

It's all because Alex is cute... ♥

It's cool, you working as a gas station attendant on weekends.

Uh, Tommy... I've got to go. I have another call. Bye!

Kat... what's wrong?

Slow down, I don't understand anything.

Can I have those?

I told you I'd give you some clothes, but come back in 10 minutes, okay?

You can see I'm busy!

Julianne is friends with some girl named SARAH-JEAN, who's the sister of Nick's brother's friend...

And...?

Nick told MAX, who told LEWIS, who told Sarah-Jean, who then told my sister he...

That he... what?

That he loves yo

14

- Friday, February 2nd:

7:15pm:

I have a super busy schedule!
If cloning were more advanced, I'd totally go for that solution.
In short, I think it's almost exhausting having so many activities!
What's more, I'm meeting more and more people at school. Yesterday,
Sophie-Anne Menard, a girl from my elementary school who didn't
even like me, said hello to me!

Weirdly, the fact the Sophie-Anne would say hello to me (timidly, too)
is almost like, shall we say, personal revenge.

I'm popular... I'm popular?
Me?!? Popular! Woo-hoo!

8:00pm:

Being really busy with my homework, John's basketball practice, my
friends and my family, I haven't had much time to ponder this:
❤ ❤ ❤ Nick still loves me! ❤ ❤ ❤ ❤
In fact, I think I've been totally stunned the last few days
by that news. I can't believe it... He still ♥ me?

Okay, let's be clear (well, let it be clear to me), I love John.
He's so cool. He's handsome, kind, awesome, marvelous,
and he has magnificent tendons behind his knees.

8:08pm:

With John, it's not love like with Nick. I don't spend my time wanting
to breathe in his scent or wanting to save his chewing gum.
. And nothing's going "teeleeteelee" in my head.

With him, I sometimes can't control my brain anymore,
but it's that way with all the boys I meet. The best thing
with John is that he's helping me make new friends.
. I like the girls Kat calls "parakeets."

And the fact that Frederica (one of the parakeets) is John's ex
doesn't bother me. They're friends. It's kind of like me and Nick!

Hurray for maturity!

Saturday, February 3rd, 9:34pm

Pfff. I had an image of him tonight that totally traumatized me...

Maybe the closer you get with someone the more you feel comfortable and that's a good sign...?

Hmm, I'm not so sure?

6:30pm

It's really nice of your parents to invite me over for dinner.

They wanted to meet you.

Hey, here's my brat of a sister.

Hi, AUDREY!

John, let me sit there.

Uh... it's Amy.

Kids... dinner time!

Here, have a seat.

Hey! You're gross! You farted on it!

Poot!

I don't know how girls your age could want to date my brother...

He's just a big idiot!

Do you like oysters, Amy?

Uh... well... not really

16

The Emperor Napoleon kept the English from supplying themselves in the lands of the Baltic Sea...

What a dictator! He reminds me of my mom!

She refuses to let me get supplies in malls! I need new clothes to become more of a woman...

EMPEROR NAPOLEO

Hey... you got a thing for the boy in the science club...

Go on, fess up!

Why don't you ask John to have a party at his house on Friday... that way I could invite Alex!

A little quiet, please!

EMPEROR NAPOLEON

I'll talk to him after school.

Cool!

I'll save seats in the cafeteria.

Okay, coming!

Hi!

Oh... hi!

Ever since Kat told me the "gossip," I really haven't tried to be in touch with Nick. It makes me uncomfortable knowing he's still in love with me...

Friday, February 9th, 7:15pm

It was a good idea of yours to encourage me to have a party, Amy!

JOHN'S PARTY

≥SQUEEE!≤ Alex is here!

So? Have you talked to Alex?

Well... he talked to me about the advantages of science club.

≥Pfff!≤ That's all.

Why don't my plans with boys ever work out?

I don't think you should be disappointed about some moron who doesn't notice what an awesome girl you are!

Come on, let's go see JF. He looks bored.

9:05pm

My birthday is in a month, and I'd like to have some romance.

I got my heart broken last year and... blablabla...

Kat's been telling him her life story for ten minutes. I feel like the two of them really get along. I'll leave them be.

Come on, Amy. Let's dance!

It's cool having new friends.

10:10am

*A sports complex in Montreal.

19

You know Denise Patry, one of Frank's most important clients, loved you yesterday.

I'm really proud of you, hon.

Little Anthony is nice!

- Wednesday, February 14th:

Huge blizzard yesterday. School's closed. I spent my day sending email....

It's February 14th and It's ... tatatataaa Valentine's Day!

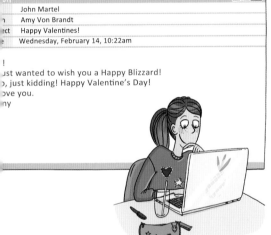

	John Martel
	Amy Von Brandt
...ect	Happy Valentines!
	Wednesday, February 14, 10:22am

...just wanted to wish you a Happy Blizzard!
...o, just kidding! Happy Valentine's Day!
...ove you.
...ny

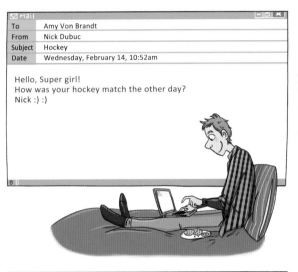

To	Amy Von Brandt
From	Nick Dubuc
Subject	Hockey
Date	Wednesday, February 14, 10:52am

Hello, Super girl!
How was your hockey match the other day?
Nick :) :)

	Nick Dubuc
...m	Amy Von Brandt
...ect	RE: Hockey
	Wednesday, February 14, 10:54am

...was cool! I've discovered an unsuspected passion
...r hockey! And I even took a ride around the rink on
...e Zamboni... Crazy!
...ny ;)

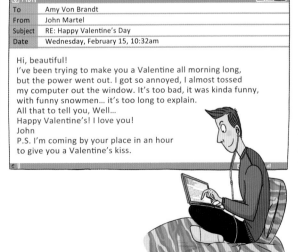

To	Amy Von Brandt
From	John Martel
Subject	RE: Happy Valentine's Day
Date	Wednesday, February 15, 10:32am

Hi, beautiful!
I've been trying to make you a Valentine all morning long,
but the power went out. I got so annoyed, I almost tossed
my computer out the window. It's too bad, it was kinda funny,
with funny snowmen... it's too long to explain.
All that to tell you, Well...
Happy Valentine's! I love you!
John
P.S. I'm coming by your place in an hour
to give you a Valentine's kiss.

Thursday, February 15th, 8:13am

You know, yesterday afternoon, John braved the blizzard to come see me!

Cool!

Not really! When he arrived, Sybil rubbed against him while purring. John started sneezing, got red blotches all over his face... he's allergic to cats!

Not coo

Hey! Are you waiting for me, Amy?

Did I eat any peanut butter this morning or not?

≠Whew!≠ No!

I want a boyfriend, too!

Kat, see you in class, okay?

≠Pfff!≠ John's here. I don't exist anymore.

Oops!

22

24

It moved all by itself!

- Thursday, March 1st:

5:52pm:
I think choosing a deodorant is the most complicated thing in the universe! Am I more "wild berry"? "Funny melon"? "Gourmet strawberry"? Or "springtime breeze"? ..."Morning freshness," maybe?

It's really hard!!!!!

I'd love for my life to already be written down in a book (that wouldn't have been written by me) so I could consult it at times when I have choices to make. I'd just have to look twenty pages later. Or even at the end, that way, I'd know what to do as a career.

And I'd know what to do about my love-life!

I wouldn't have to make any decisions, because everything would be decided in advance. I wouldn't be forced to invent the next part myself. Let's just say it would be relaxing!

That would also keep me from having surprises. For example, if I'd known my dad was going to die, I could've prepared myself for it. We could've spent his final moments together...

And if I'd known Tommy was going to kiss me in front of the windows of MusicPlus, last year, I wouldn't have gone there. Maybe I'd still be dating Nick now. But I wouldn't have my marvelous friend Tommy.

6:02pm:
Without any great conviction, I chose "wild berry." Simply because it's the deodorant stick I had in my hands when the cosmetics saleswoman suspiciously scowled at me, like: "You're a teenager, so you're probably going to steal something." Pfffffffffffff!

Hair spider!

- Friday, March 2nd, 10:10am:
Awkward... Nick and I pretend not to see each other by the lockers...

Saturday, March 3rd, 9:00am

Stop pouting!

You'll have plenty of time to see your friends next week during the break.

I don't want to spend my weekend with Frank's parents. And I don't want to leave Sybil all alone.

A cat can be by itself for 2 days... Come on, get in the car.

Yes, but Kat, Tommy, JF, and I wanted to play videogames.

9:34am

Nick kissed me... and I didn't really know how to react...

My mouth, probably because that's what it has to do when another mouth approaches... moved... to kiss his mouth.

I really wish I could've escaped before Tommy kissed me, I didn't see it coming. But with Nick, I saw it coming. And I sat there, and my mouth moved... My mouth MOVED! (It's weighing on me).

Maybe I really do have problems with brain functions and I'm not always in control of each of my limbs. Yes, that's the only explanation.

I told John about the kiss. He asked me if I still loved Nick. I told him no, that he, John, was the one I loved. He took me in his arms and we kissed. He forgives more easily than Nick!

- Sunday, March 4th, 9:00am:

Aaaargh!

While washing my hair this morning, I screamed, there was a huge spider in the bathtub... Frank's mom ran into the bathroom. And since there was no lock, she saw me completely naked!!!! Aaaargh! In fact, the spider was a ball of my hair. Real smart! And we almost couldn't escape this isolated chalet out in the country. There was a snowstorm, but fine, we got on the road to come home. And tomorrow is spring break! Yippee! :)

Monday, March 5th, 11:00am

Life's perfect when there's no school or family activities on the schedule.

I totally feel like being a slacker. This afternoon, a movie with my new girlfriends.

Kat refused to come with us. Is she being jealous, I wonder?

1:00pm

You know what, Sybil? John invited me to go skiing along with his parents and little sister on Wednesday.

Me telling him I'm not very athletic did no good. He insisted...

≥Pfff.≤ What will I wear?

2:41pm

Ha ha ha!

Hee hee hee!

Ha ha ha!

Hee hee hee!

Ha ha ha!

5:00pm

Are you coming over?

We'll watch videos on YouTube.

Sure, cool!

I didn't see the time when I left Roxanne's, but it was past 7pm. My mom was furious I got home so late without calling her. And like usual, she was worried. She said to me: "I bought you a cellphone, if it's always going to be out of power, what use is it?"

28

30

Happy Birthday!

You're just getting here now?

Uh... I told you I was going to see John's basketball game, I left at halftime!

What'd you get for my sister?

Go to your bedroom, Julianne!

It's MY birthday. You have no business being here!

Happy Birthday!

Oh! Thanks!

I'm gonna tell Mom you kissed a boy!

JF and... Kat?!

They're dating?

Well... if you didn't spend so much time with your other friends, you'd know that!

But how? When?

Why? Kat always tells me everything!

I guess not.

33

Leaving Kat's place, I dialed John's number on my cellphone, but he wasn't there. Then I saw Tommy coming towards me and I told him what happened. He said that he'd heard everything, that I was mean when I said JF had a 50s haircut. But Kat had just told me my boyfriend had poodle hair.

Me

Ex best friend 4 ever

John →

Perfect timing

Happy Easter

- Monday, April 2nd:

6:30pm:
Kat was right. Frederica's still totally in love with John. Whenever she looks at him, her eyes shine... I wonder if they haven't already kissed each other since their breakup, kind of like me with Nick. And they wouldn't have told me. And that would be the reason John didn't get mad when I told him about my kiss with Nick...

7:02pm:
I imagined my future with John.
① I'd spend my time watching basketball games and/or soccer matches.
② I'd spend my time with his friends because he doesn't want to leave his group to come see mine.
③ A life without peanut butter and without Sybil (because of his allergies).

I really like John, but I have the distinct impression there's NO room for me.

How long can a relationship go on once you discover it has no future?

8:10pm: DRAMA!!!!!

My mom broke up with Frank and quit her job (she works in Frank's company). She told me, (stuck to a box of Kleenex and pulling out tissue after tissue while crying), that her love for my father was still there. Frank would like things to progress between them, like, living together.
But my mom isn't ready, she told me (sniffling):
"How could I go any further since I still love someone else?
Who isn't here anymore?..."
And I told her: "I'm probably going to break up with John, too..."

And then she took me in her arms and said: "I love you."

I miss Kat...

I've got a strong desire for chocolate. It's becoming an obsession.

Wednesday, April 4th, 4:30pm

I don't know how to tell John it's over between us.

Friday, April 6th, 6:17pm

I'm through with PTA. It's no fun.

The teachers have noticed a loss of interest in class, and in math you're a disaster.

I've given you lots of freedom.

I thought you were responsible. Yc promised me you'd make an effort!

Do you want to end up as a cashier... is that what you want?

You're such a snob!

There's nothing wrong with being a cashier!

And besides, I'll never be a cashier 'cause I...

SUCK AT MATH!

SLAM

My mom really was a lot cooler when she had a boyfriend.

36

Poem

My friend for life

You were my friend
Now we're torn asunder
I'd love to talk to you
But you refuse to listen

Is there anything left of our friendship?
Or has it all been erased?
Have we become strangers?
Is our friendship forever lost?

I'm afraid an awkwardness has grown between us
And that things will never be the same
Living without each other hurts us
But we continue to ignore one another.

Who, in fact, is right?
What use is it asking that question?
Will it change anything, after all?
I just hope we'll be together again one day.

- Kat & Me -

Best Friends 4 ever!

Sunday, April 8th, 10:27am

Did you get my Easter egg?

Oh! BRAD, I love you so much.

Yes! But it's a lot smaller than last year.

Yes, but since I know you overindulge in chocolate...

Oh, but I'm doing a lot better, you know... I'm resisting!

ASHLEY, I love you, too... but I love CINDY, also...

I'm leaving John today.

Tuesday, April 10th, 5:01pm

I like you a lot, but maybe more as a friend than as a boyfriend...

Yeah, I understand. I was thinking that, too.

5:30pm

In the end, it went really well, fast, like a lightning bolt.

5:35pm

Okay, now, I've got to go by Frank's office to tell him it's kind of my fault Mom left him.

6:10pm

You know, at first, I didn't really like you... but now, I do... and you're the only person who's brought any light to my mom's eyes since before my dad's death... I know she loves you...

If you still love her, you just have to tell her... in a romantic way!

So, it turns out you don't like me not being around anymore?

Hee hee hee!

Ha ha ha!!

39

Wednesday, April 11th, 12:35pm

Have you heard the news?

Frederica's dating John again!

But wasn't he dating Amy Von Brandt?

They broke up!

She didn't waste any time from what I can tell.

12:55pm

I hope you're not mad at me... and that we'll stay friends...

No way! Uh... not "no, we won't stay friends," no, I'm not mad at you.

Me and John were a... period thing... uh... periodic thing! It only lasted three months... So, okay, I wish you both a happy reunion!

Thanks!

I've lost everything... even Kat!

She's probably forgotten me.

She can't forget you when you're in class together. You dope!

Kat misses you as much as you miss her. You girls are so proud.

What do you know about girls, Mr. I-spend-my-life-in-my-basement?

40

41

Saturday, April 21st, 3:00pm

We're leaving. It's the only solution, Sybil.

Nick won't talk to me anymore. Kat and I are totally history. It's over with John, and I don't see Frederica, Nadia, and Roxanne anymore.

Nothing's keeping me here!

Goodbye, Mom. Goodbye, Frank.

Moving: no thanks. I'm going to go live with Granny Von Brandt. Call me to tell me your new address (that'll be handy when I come to get the rest of my stuff).

Wishing you both happiness,
Amy
XOXO

BUS DEPOT

5:00pm

5:30pm

What an idiot. My cellphone fell into the station toilet right as I flushed it...

≋PFFF!≋ ...NOW I DON'T HAVE A CELLPHONE!

43

8:40pm

Tommy! What are you doing here?

I thought you'd need a friend.

How did you get here?

With your mom, what did you think?

That we'd let you leave without doing anything?

So, if I understand correctly, you plan to move here, far from everybody you love?

Well... uh...

Amy! I don't want you to move so far away...

What do I have left back there?

Me!

Oh, no! Awkward, awkward! He loves me!

Tommy, the two of us just isn't possible. I love when you play the guitar, but you annoy me most of the time...

So, it'll never work.

What are you talking about? You had something in your hair, and I didn't want to tell you so you wouldn't freak out.

...AAAAAAAH!

Kat and me = BFF forever and ever and ever.

- Friday, May 4th:

6:09pm:

It's been a week since Kat and I made up.
I went to see her with the poem I wrote for her about
friendship. We hugged each other, we cried, we laughed, we apologized.
And then we updated each other about our lives. She knew about
my breakup with John (Tommy's the one who'd told her), she
told me about JF. Things are cool with them. It's not passionate
like with JD, it's a love based more on great friendship.

Everything's back to normal!!!!! Yeah!

I had the feeling, these past months, I was living somebody
else's life and that I'd finally found my own again.

FENG SHUI

7:10pm:

I've seen the house Mom and Frank picked out. They did show it
to me, however, before making the official purchase offer on it (what
generosity!). It's nice. Nothing more. I'm not crazy about the colors.
And I think the room layout isn't too feng shui. (I often go to the
dentist's, and there's nothing but decorating magazines to read.
I'm awesome in feng shui now!). So, the house isn't really my thing.

BEST
SANDWICH IN
THE UNIVERSE

- Saturday, May 5th, 8:20am:

Today I have a job interview at 9:45 at a restaurant where they
make sandwiches. Not that I was particularly wanting to work;
my mom's forcing me into this. Basically, she told me having
a job would make me more independent and would let me buy
whatever I want... she's not wrong!

If I work at a sandwich shop, maybe it'll become my gang's hangout.
Like, everyone will come there and talk to me while I clean
the counter. Maybe my bosses will even think I'm increasing
their clientele.

Beeeeep
Beeeeeeeep
7:00
Beeeeeeeep!

I think that, overall, it went well. I left the office after shaking Mr. Lalonde's hand once more and his assistant's hand. Under the heading of "Other useful information about you," I'd put: I love to walk while dragging my feet on the street in the fall, when there are leaves that carpet the ground. I love to pop the bubbles in bubble wrap and I hate stepping on chewing gum. I did my best (even if I can't affirm beyond all doubt that's entirely pertinent for a job interview!).

47

48

49

Sunday, May 27th, 1:15pm

≠Pfff!≠ I'd have rather seen Kat this afternoon. She's hurting because of JF, after all.

Oh, my baby bonnet... yuck, it smells moldy!

1:45pm

Yoohoo! Your mom let me in!

Kat? It was cool of you to come.

You okay? Are things fine between you and JF?

Yeah... you know, I can't be mad at him. He's probably the boy I love the most in the world.

I don't want to lose him, but it hurts all the same.

Oh... Kat... Do like I do and date the poster of a famous actor. Or enter the sect of single people I just created.

Will you help me take down all my stars from the ceiling?

Leave them there! Just figure the new owners will come and paint the room... it's too annoying taking down all the stars!

Ahhh! Yes! Great idea!

Ha ha ha!

54

JUNE
A Change of Pace

- Friday, June 1st:

6:03pm:

I can really feel the end of the school year coming! Everyone's a little excited in anticipation. Summer's just around the corner, even though it's overcast and rainy. It's like a lull, just before the exam week, when you already almost feel like you're on vacation and when you forget you have big-time studying to do.

6:08pm:

Kat and JF are stuck together like never before. There's no awkwardness between them. It was a shock at first, but she's happy JF's being honest with himself. The ONLY problem is that Frederica heard the conversation in the Sandwich Shop, and I think she told a few people, because JF's getting weird looks at school. But since he's quick-witted (he is!), he stands up for himself. We talked a lot with JF, it drew all four of us closer together. He explained to us he really did feel in love with Kat. That he feels like she's his soulmate. But his nature caught up with him. And that it wasn't his fault.

6:35pm:

I'm going to miss my friends... everyone's going their separate ways for summer vacation. Kat's spending several weeks at her horse-riding camp. JF's going on a trip with his parents, and Tommy's going to his mom's...

Several endings are approaching. The end of the school year. The end of spring. The end of my life in MY house. The end of the world, too, perhaps? Naaah, I'm kidding! **I don't really want to move!!!!!!**

Amy's Room

7:00pm:

Yesterday, we had a food fight in the cafeteria. While leaning over to pick up a few pieces of bread on the ground, I bumped heads with someone else... Nick. I suddenly felt out of breath, my heart started throbbing. But I think it was because of the food fight that had exhausted me and for saying stupid things in Nick's presence such as:
"Sorry... Oops... Uh-oh..."

HAPPY BIRTHDAY
JULIANNE!!!   LADY

May I come in...? I'd like for both of us to talk.

So, I know moving is very stressful, and that's why we get mad sometimes.

I hate when she runs her hand through my hair... I'm not a baby anymore.

But I'll control myself and let her do it!

You know, the other evening, when you told me you wished I'd never met Frank and that you'd prefer we stayed here the rest of our lives not to betray the memory of your dad... that hurt me.

I said that in anger. I know... sometimes I get carried away and--

And you can't stay angry with me!

Why not?

Because tomorrow I'm taking you to see your favorite band!

WHAT?! My... favorite band!

60

Tuesday, June 12th, 7:02pm

— Friday, June 15th:
End-of-year ceremony. Trophies are awarded to students who've distinguished themselves by the scholarly and athletic excellence or by their personality.

I hope I get a prize!!!!

9:02pm

Good job, JF, for the prize for the most distinguished look... and now I'd like to award the prize for initiative and creativity to...

clap clap clap clap clap

AWARDS FOR EXCELLENCE

Amy Von Brandt...

For her idea for a yoga class!

Good job, honey!

clap clap clap

AWARDS FOR EXCELLENCE

9:08pm

You just dropped something...

Don't trip... don't trip...

AWARDS FOR EXCELLENCE

An orphaned sock that must have been stuck inside your skirt.

HA HA HA HA HA HA HA HA HA

AWARDS FOR EXCELLENCE

The sock of shame!

63

The sock of shame!!!

- Sunday, July 1st   :

Lots of things happened after the episode of the fallen sock on stage.
But okay, I came out of it all right! It let me solve an enigma:
Now I know there's no ghost in the washing machine...
It's just static electricity making the clothes stick together.

Okay, I really did get
embarrassed in front of everyone!   Weeteepeewoopeedoowooahhhhhh!
                                          School's over!!!!!

My last night in my house... was last night. I finished packing my last
box at 9:52pm exactly. Tommy came over to help me. I felt a little
sad... I had tears in my eyes looking at the stars on the ceiling...
I thought back to everything I'd experienced in my house... important
details about my dad. The other day, my mom told me he had hair in his
ears and, in my memories, he didn't have any. (Maybe it was a single
hair, maybe in her memory, she added some... How can I trust
my mom's memory?).

Award for
Initiative
and
Creativity

That's what will happen to me with my home. I'll forget. And certain
memories I'd sometimes have, flashbacks that came to me just
because I was in the house, will maybe no longer come to mind.
Moving means forgetting my dad even more.

Moving
Truck

8:23am:
This morning, the huge moving truck arrived. Then
everything was emptied from my home.

And I watched that huge truck drive off with all of our stuff.
And then I felt like my home, empty, wasn't really my home anymore.

10:30am:
That's it, I'm in Frank's car, Sybil's cage on my lap, boxes beside me...
I'm having trouble breathing. I swore I wouldn't look back or look
at Tommy, who's waving at me.

Okay, I'm moving two streets away... it's not the far side of
the world, after all! But starting now, nothing will ever
be like it was before.

FRAGILE

— Thursday, July 5th:

Our house is starting to feel like a home. Tommy left for vacation the day before yesterday, so I'm the only one from our group here. This weekend, we're going to see my Collier grandparents at the campground. Frank decided we'd camp out, that there was no way we'd sleep in my grandparents RV. I don't really like camping out... that means there'll be critters... littles one, big ones...

Mom, your breakfast was yummy!

Okay, let's go into the forest to set up our tent.

3:01pm

Is it far away?

Here... it's perfect for putting up the tent.

3:35pm

What do we do now?

It's an adventure! We're not slaves to time here.

Enjoy it and breat in the fresh ai

68

3:40pm

Breathing...

3:47pm

Breathing...

3:48pm

Yeah, it smells good...

Okay, I'm done breathing the fresh air... and now I don't have anything left to do!

What, you're finished?

You can't be done with breathing!

Hoo hoo hoo!

10:24pm

Clik clik...

Nok nok...

Hoo hoo hoo!

I need to pee... but there's so much noise!

shooo oo...

Krak

CRUNCH

69

72

Dear 11:11. I'd like to thank you for setting Rick on my path. I realize these past few years I've made some totally pointless wishes, but tonight, if Rick and I could just kiss, I'd think you were really extra cool for the rest of my life.

Thanks ♥

P.S.: Keep leeches far away from me, if you have time.

9:17pm

Adopt a nonchalant attitude... I mustn't seem like I've been counting the minutes all day long!

Ah, Amy!

I'll introduce my friends! That's VALERIE and her boyfriend VICTOR.

Hi!

Hi!

DAMIEN, my camping buddy, and ZACHARY, my little brother.

That's cool. You're star-gazing?

Hey, BLOUIN!

Give her a break with your stars!

No, no, it's fine. I like the stars!

10:47pm

Rick's last name is Blouin.

Amy Blouin. Amy Von Brandt-Blouin or Amy Blouin-Von Brandt?

73

Dear 11:11, Honestly,
I don't think you're very fast!
I'm still waiting....
for Rick to kiss me!

Hey, there, surprise! Your mom invited me to spend the weekend with you all!

Kaaat!

And look who's here, too?

Meeeow!

Friday, July 13th, 10:30am

WELCOME TO THE CAMPGROUND

2:04pm

Amy, come swim!

Uh... not now!

Kat and Rick really seem to have hit it off...

I'm jealous!

Saturday, July 14th, 11:10pm

Nooo, it's not true!

And here I thought Rick was my cosmic soulmate!

74

- Friday, August 3rd:

9:05pm:
The end of my vacation at the campground really sucked!
When I saw Kat kissing Rick... I don't know what got into me, surely
out of spite... I kissed Damien. When I think back on it, it gives me
spasms of fright. I kissed him and it really was totally disgusting!
(I still get the shivers)... He had a doughy mouth and bad
breath (it almost tasted like the smell of manure).

I'm trying to forget that moment which has been on a loop in my
mind for days and makes me gag.

And that evening, in the RV, Kat confided to me that Rick had
told her: "I'm Amy's cosmic soulmate, but I'm in love with you
by mistake, Kat!" No, he didn't say that. She simply told me that
no boy had ever had that effect on her. That no boy had ever
kissed her like that!
I'm jealous of my friend and I'm mad at myself!

We celebrated my birthday on July 17th at the campground. But my heart
wasn't in it! Okay, I did get a bicycle as a gift! The only nice thing: Tommy
sang a song to me over the phone. My mom told me she wanted to organize
a surprise party with my friends... and then she gave up because it was too
difficult to invite my friends to the campground. Then we came home
on July 20th.

- Saturday, August 4th, 2:30pm:
I woke up this morning with a start. A frightened Sybil had
jumped on me.

Booooooo!!!

I don't really like sleeping in the basement... I realize that now.
I think that if ghosts existed, they'd live in the basement.
Not only because of the laundry room, but because it's a chilly,
humid, terrifying place... and there are spiders there, too.

It's decided, I don't want to sleep here anymore!

- Thursday, August 16th:

Kat misses Rick and wants to introduce him to her parents. Yesterday, it seems, on the phone, they said to each other: "I love you" (awful big news). So Rick's been invited to dinner at Kat's Saturday. So she asked me to be there. Awesome! (Pffff!) I've decided to stop being out of sorts. Because, frankly, it's been getting on my nerves bigtime for a while now. I had "the revelation" this morning in the shower.

Shampoo twice while massaging your hair 2 to 3 minutes and savor that moment of gentleness...

I'm fed up with attaching too much importance to everything. I always brag about being super-Zen and I'm always creating a tempest in a teapot... I need gentleness!

I'll get mad at Nick instead of with my mom. If Nick thinks I'm a loser because my mom invited him to my birthday party, he's the one with a problem!

Saturday, August 18th, 8:30pm

How will they sustain their love since they're not in the same school and not even in the same neighborhood?

I live a half-hour by bicycle from your house and I'll start with my learner's permit, that way Kat and I could see each other often.

I'm not about to let my daughter ride off at night on a bike all alone and I certainly won't let her get into a car with a boy!

It's crazy... I have telepathic abilities!

79

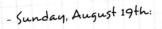

- Sunday, August 19th:

ARGHHH!!!! I ran into Nick at the water park. I got my hair tangled up in my glow bracelet (that they make us wear to prove we've paid the entrance fee) when I tried to make a little gesture to tell him hello. Then I stumbled with my flipflops while walking towards him. I told him it was nice seeing him again... and I left to rejoin Tommy, Kat, JF, and Rick. What a fiasco!

Monday, April 20th, 12:02pm

Dingdingding!

Awwww... I was sleeping so well!

12:05pm

Uh...

I...

May I come in?

12:07pm

Your mom invited me to your birthday...

I'm going to wake up. I'm in the middle of a nightmare!

I'm sorry about my mom. She didn't know we weren't talking to each other anymore. She was trying to surprise me.

Yes... that's why I told her I couldn't come.

I figured you wouldn't want to see me.

Here, I'm a month late for your birthday!

It's dried food for astronauts. I ordered it on the internet. It's for all the times your "head's in the clouds."

In a few days, I'll start my final year in high school... I don't really know what awaits me afterwards. Maybe I just have to stop fearing the unknown and let myself be surprised, to manage the present. Sometimes, I feel like everything's always starting over. As though I were always rebuilding foundations atop ruins and that, time after time, storms were blowing away my work. But through everything I've experienced, I've understood one thing: regardless of what I do to struggle against it, my heart will always be stronger than me.

Welcome to AMY'S DIARY #3 "Moving On," based on the novels by India Desjardins, adapted by Véronique Grisseaux, writer, and Laëtitia Aynié, artist. Unlike many long-running comicbook characters, Amy Von Brandt is growing older with each and every volume of this graphic novel series. How could she not? This series is based upon her diaries, after all. We get to see Amy's life unfold, and we witness all of her ups and downs, her smart decisions and her mistakes. It's a fascinating look at the life of a teenage girl just trying to lead as happy a life as possible, despite certain problems.

In AMY'S DIARY #1 "Space Alien…Almost?" it was revealed that Amy copes with perhaps her greatest problem, the loss of her father, by imagining that he's "not gone, but an extraterrestrial who returned to his planet." Obviously, Amy knows that's not really true, but a fiction she's telling herself to cope with her tragic loss. But what if it was true? What if AMY'S DIARY was a science fiction series, and we found out what did happen to her father? Well, Charmz happens to be an imprint of Papercutz, which also has another imprint called Super Genius. There's a graphic novel series published by Papercutz and one by Super Genius that may explore that kind of territory.

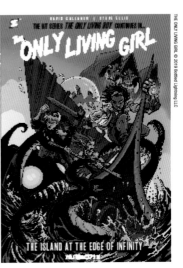

First there's Zandra Parfitt, THE ONLY LIVING GIRL, co-created by writer, David Gallaher, and artist, Steve Ellis. Zee, as she's usually called, first appeared in THE ONLY LIVING BOY, the Harvey Award-nominated series by Gallaher and Ellis, which has been collected by Papercutz into a beautiful OMNIBUS edition. The ONLY LIVING GIRL series stars Zee, who after years of being in suspended animation, has woken up on a strange new world and is now haunted by memories of her past. As the only living girl she must redeem her lost father's legacy, while trying to survive life on this strange planet. If Amy was aware of what Zee was going through, she'd probably want to rethink the whole my-father-was-taken-by-aliens scenario. Just take a look at the preview pages starting on the next page, for a taste of exactly what Zee is going through (and some hints at exactly why she needs to redeem her father's legacy).

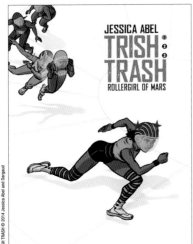

Then there's Patricia "Trish Trash" Nupindju, who was actually born on Mars—200 years in the future. Her parents weren't exactly taken away by aliens, but by something far more sinister. Trish is seven and a half in Martian years, which is 15 in Earth years. She dreams of becoming the biggest hoverderby star on Mars, as it seems the only way to escape a future of poverty and hard labor on her family's moisture farm in Candor Chasma. But even if she could make the team, she's too young to get a pro hoverderby contract. What's a girl to do? Trish's whole story was told in three great Eisner Award-nominated graphic novels, TRISH TRASH ROLLERGIRL OF MARS by writer/artist Jessica Abel. All three graphic novels are available separately or in one big COLLECTED EDITION from Super Genius. Check out the short preview starting right after THE ONLY LIVING GIRL preview. Life on Mars is certainly not something we imagine Amy would want to experience.

Meanwhile back on Earth, Amy continues her unique journey and hopes you'll pick up AMY'S DIARY #4 "Secret Plan," coming soon to your favorite bookseller or library. While she may not want anyone else to read her diary, she's willing to make an exception for you. Sorry, but AMY'S DIARY is currently unavailable on Mars.

Thanks,

Jim

Editor-in-Chief

STAY IN TOUCH!

EMAIL: salicrup@papercutz.com
WEB: Papercutz.com
TWITTER: @papercutzgn
INSTAGRAM: @papercutzgn
FACEBOOK: PAPERCUTZGRAPHICNOVELS
FANMAIL: Charmz, 160 Broadway, Suite 700, East Wing, New York, NY 10038

I LEARNED EVERYTHING I COULD FROM MY FATHER.

I KNOW QUITE A BIT ABOUT GRAVITY AND YOU SEEM TO KNOW A COUPLE OF THINGS ABOUT SCIENCE AND STUFF.

"MAKE EVERY DAY JEALOUS OF YESTERDAY" WAS HIS MOTTO.

ON THOSE BLEAK NIGHTS WHEN MY FATHER WOULD WORK LATE...

...I BROUGHT MY IDEAS TO LIFE.

MY ONLY LIMITS...

DONT WALK

...WERE THE DARK RECESSES OF MY IMAGINATION.

SURE, I MADE MISTAKES.

COME ON, JUPITER, YOU KNOW YOUR ORBIT ISN'T *THAT* LOW.

BUT THEY WERE *MY* MISTAKES TO MAKE.

DONT WALK

AND I MADE A LOT OF THEM.

BUT I ALWAYS TRIED TO LEARN FROM THEM.

SOME MISTAKES STICK WITH YOU.

THESE LIGHTS, HUH?

YEAH. THEY TAKE FOREVER.

SOME MISTAKES HAUNT YOU.

Continued in THE ONLY LIVING GIRL #1, available now at booksellers and libraries.

Special Bonus Preview of
TRISH TRASH ROLLERGIRL OF MARS #1...

...here comes Betty Demonica...

...nice block by Deb O'Station...

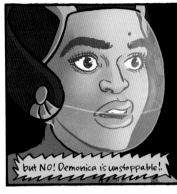

but NO! Demonica is unstoppable!

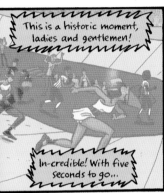

This is a historic moment, ladies and gentlemen!

In-credible! With five seconds to go...

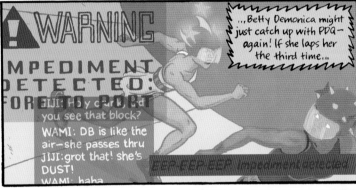

WARNING

IMPEDIMENT DETECTED: FOREIGN ROBOT

...Betty Demonica might just catch up with PDQ— again! If she laps her the third time...

EEP·EEP·EEP·Impediment Detected

...you see that block?
WAMI: DB is like the air—she passes thru
JIJI: grot that! she's DUST!
WAMI: haha

Un-be-lieve-able! Betty Demonica, the league high-scorer, has just scored 19 points in one jam!

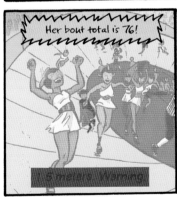

Her bout total is 76!

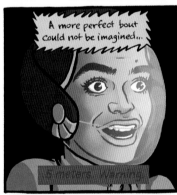

A more perfect bout could not be imagined...

Crap.

GRIINDDDD

TRIX: where are you guys?
WAMI: yr not here? open tryout TNs.

Open tryout?

WAMI: well, open to 9 and up!
THORSON: hahaha
YONTAK: baby trix!

How did I not know this?

"Baby." I'm seven and a half.*

JIJI: U wouldn't get in anyway. crowded.
TRIX: grot u guyz. thx for telling me!

USER TRIX LOGGED OFF

5:43

Skate like a nine-year-old.

USER TRIX LOGGED OFF

And I'm like ten klicks from the grotted house.

*That's fifteen in Earth years. Martian years are twice as long as those on Earth.

I hate this dirtball plaaaaaneeeet!

Continued in TRISH TRASH ROLLERGIRL OF MARS #1 or TRISH TRASH THE COLLECTED EDITION, available now at booksellers and libraries.